W9-CMS-786

THE RIGHT HONOURABLE THE LORD MAYOR
SIR CHRISTOPHER COLLETT GBE MA

THE MANSION HOUSE LONDON EC4N 8BH
TELEPHONE 01·626 2500

I welcome the opportunity to introduce this new edition of John Burningham's delightful book, which has given the greatest pleasure to countless readers, including my family and myself, who know and love the City of London.

The year 1989 marks a very special year for the City of London and its local authority, The Corporation of London, as it is the 800th Anniversary of the appointment of London's first Mayor, Henry Fitz Alwyn. An event which will be marked by my creation of the Lord Mayor's 800th Anniversary Awards Trust, which will provide scholarships and grants for special projects for young people upon whom the future depends.

This edition of Humbert is a splendid memento of the celebration of 800 unbroken years of a unique and great office, for the Lord Mayor's Show still takes place each year, now on the second Saturday in November, when the new Lord Mayor is shown to the citizens of London, and is sworn in before Her Majesty's Judges at the Law Courts. He travels there in a golden coach, but you never know what may happen, and one day Humbert's chance may come.

LORD MAYOR

HUMBERT

MISTER FIRKIN

&

THE LORD MAYOR

OF LONDON

written and illustrated
by
JOHN BURNINGHAM

Crown Publishers, Inc.
New York

To Scrap Dealers, Brewers, Coal Merchants,
Lord Mayors, & all who continue to use horses

Copyright © 1965 by John Burningham
Introduction copyright © 1989 by Christopher Collett

Published in 1989 in the United States of America by Crown Publishers,
Inc., 225 Park Avenue South, New York, New York 10003

Published in Great Britain by Jonathan Cape Ltd

CROWN is a trademark of Crown Publishers, Inc.

Manufactured in Great Britain

Library of Congress Catalog Card Number: 68-1228

Library of Congress Cataloging-in-Publication Data
Burningham, John. Humbert, Mister Firkin & the Lord Mayor of
London/written and illustrated by John Burningham.
p.   cm.
Summary: An old cart horse and his master rescue the Lord Mayor when
his coach breaks down and, in reward, they are invited to the Mayor's
banquet.
ISBN 0-517-57312-1 : $12.95
[1. Horses—Fiction.   2. London (England)—Fiction.] I. Title.
II. Title: Humbert, Mister Firkin and the Lord Mayor of London.
PZ7.B936Hu   1989
[E]—dc19   88-38523
CIP
AC

ISBN 0-517-57312-1

10 9 8 7 6 5 4 3 2 1

First Crown Edition

Humbert was a working horse. He worked with Mr Firkin who was a scrap-iron dealer, and they used to travel round the streets of London. Mr Firkin would shout out: "Any scrap, any old iron, lead or copper for sale?"

They lived in a small street where Humbert
had a stable on the ground floor and Mr Firkin
had the rooms above.

Every day Humbert and Mr Firkin set out early

to start collecting the scrap. Mr Firkin used to keep to the quieter streets as much as possible so as not to meet too much traffic which Humbert did not like.

Humbert had a friend who lived a few doors
down. He was a horse that pulled a cart full of
flowers and shrubs, and whenever Humbert had a
chance he would take a bite as his friend pulled
the cart past the stable door.

Mr Firkin and Humbert
travelled through dockland
sometimes. Humbert liked
the smells of food there.

He knew how to be nice to children, who would give him things to eat, and if he was lucky he would even get an apple.

Humbert liked apples.

Now Mr Firkin often stopped for lunch in a pub that was near a brewery. There were lots of horses there, and as he knew the man who looked after them, Mr Firkin used to leave Humbert in the stable yard.

The brewery horses were much bigger than Humbert, and they were terrible snobs. They had everything they wanted, including an annual holiday in the country. Their harnesses sparkled with polish and they were groomed every day. They were always boasting about the fact that they pulled the Lord Mayor's golden coach. "All *you* do is to pull scrap iron," they would say.

One autumn day, Mr Firkin left Humbert in the brewery yard while he had his lunch. There was a lot of commotion going on there. Six of the horses were being groomed and fitted out with the smartest harnesses Humbert had ever seen.

Humbert asked them what was going on. "Don't you know?" they said. "We're going to pull the Lord Mayor's coach tomorrow."

Humbert felt terrible. He stayed awake all night thinking how unfair life was.

He brooded about it all next morning as he and
Mr Firkin travelled through the streets. "Those
brewery horses have all the luck," he said to him-
self. He thought about his own shabby harness and
the old cart. Although Mr Firkin was very kind,
and brushed him down, kept his stable clean and
gave him plenty of food, Humbert still felt envious,
disgruntled and miserable.

Then suddenly, as they rounded a corner, down
at the end of the street they saw a huge crowd, and
Humbert rushed forward and nosed his way in
between the people to see what it was they were
looking at.

The crowd were watching none other than the Lord Mayor's Show, and there, before Humbert's eyes, came the horses from the brewery, pulling the enormous golden coach with the Lord Mayor in it. Behind the coach came the pikemen.

Humbert watched enviously as the procession
moved slowly along.
Suddenly the crowd gave a gasp.

One of the rear wheels of the coach had broken. The coach toppled down and the horses came to a stop. There was a hush. Everyone was aghast.

Such a thing had never occurred in all the hundreds of years since the Show began.

Then lots of things happened all at once.

The Lord Mayor was helped down from the broken coach, and some large cars arrived to take him to the Mansion House.

"Motor cars?" he bellowed. "Unheard of. Monstrous. On an occasion like this the Lord Mayor does not ride in a motor car. Get me another coach or something."

Humbert saw his chance. He charged forward.

The policemen and Mr Firkin tried to hold him
back, but he managed to get through, and went
straight over to the Lord Mayor. "Ah, my good
horse," said the Lord Mayor, "perhaps you and
your driver would be kind enough to take me to the
Mansion House."

Everybody cheered, except the officials. They were horrified at the idea of the Lord Mayor riding on a scrap dealer's cart. But if he wanted to do so, who could prevent him?

And so the Lord Mayor climbed up on to the cart and sat down on an old gas cooker. The crowd cheered again. The other horses looked dumb-founded and shamefaced as Humbert proudly trotted along the street.

When they arrived at the Mansion House they lined up for the photographers and the reporters. Then the Lord Mayor said goodbye to Mr Firkin and Humbert, but asked them to wait for a few more minutes as he would be sending someone out with an envelope. The envelope was brought by a footman. It contained an invitation for both Humbert and Mr Firkin to attend the Lord Mayor's Banquet to be held the following week.

When the great evening came, Humbert and Mr Firkin were seated to the left of the Lord Mayor. The Prime Minister was present and all kinds of famous people. Mr Firkin felt rather embarrassed by the whole thing.

When it was over, the Lord Mayor thanked Mr Firkin and Humbert for the part they had played in getting him to the Mansion House, and he gave Humbert a special cup in memory of the occasion. He made arrangements for him to have an annual holiday like the brewery horses, and he also arranged that when Humbert gets too old to work he will be able to spend the rest of his life peacefully in the country, as all working horses should be able to do.

Humbert has never forgotten the day of the Show or the Banquet, nor has Mr Firkin. The Lord Mayor's cup stands in Humbert's stable and Mr Firkin keeps it polished.

Often when they are out collecting scrap, people still point, and say to one another: "There they go — you know — the ones that took the Lord Mayor to the Mansion House: remember?"